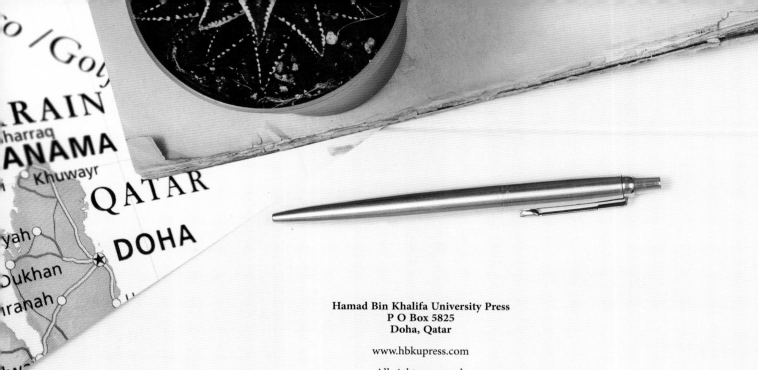

Hamad Bin Khalifa University Press
P O Box 5825
Doha, Qatar

www.hbkupress.com

DDCoral / Shutterstock.com
Ahmed Adly / Shutterstock.com
Fitria Ramli / Shutterstock.com
Fredy Thuerig / Shutterstock.com
EBONYEG / Shutterstock.com
Munzir Rosdi / Shutterstock.com
Ana Victoria Manalese / Shutterstock.com
Sven Hansche / Shutterstock.com
Imran's Photography / Shutterstock.com

First English edition in 2020

ISBN: 9789927141270

Printed in Doha, Qatar

Qatar National Library Cataloging-in-Publication (CIP)

Hayakom. First English edition. Doha, Qatar : Hamad Bin Khalifa University Press, 2020.

 pages ; cm

ISBN 978-992-714-127-0

1. Qatar -- Description and travel -- Juvenile literature. I. Hamad Bin Khalifa University Press, issuing body.

DS247.Q32 H39 2020
 953.63– dc 23   20202756602x

Omar Allouba

Mounir Slim

Ghenwa Yehia

HAYAKOM

Rima Ismail

Nikos Yanopulos

Zeyad Abuirshaid

دار جامعة حمد بن خليفة للنشر
HAMAD BIN KHALIFA UNIVERSITY PRESS

HAYAKOM
Faisal, Fadi, Rashid

Faisal

It's been way too long, guys! I can't wait for you to get to Qatar. I've got so many great things planned.

Fadi

Three hours and I'll be there! Goodbye Beirut; Doha, here I come!

Rashid

I've just arrived at Muscat International Airport. Vacation Mode ON!

ASPIRE ZONE: Located in the southern district of Doha, Qatar, it covers 88 hectares. Overlooking the park is Aspire Tower which was the tallest building in Qatar when it was built in 2006.

THE RACING & EQUESTRIAN CLUB: Built in 1975 as a tribute to Qatar's rich equestrian history. Horses were once invaluable because of the role they played in the wars and conquests that shaped the region.

DAY
2

AL KHOR PARK: One of the oldest parks in the country. It has an aviary, loads of green spaces, a waterfall, water fountains, a miniature golf course, a battery-operated train, large children's play areas, a basketball court, an amphitheater, a skating area, and a small zoo with many animals.

AL THAKHIRA: The area is known for its pristine beaches and 10km coast made of *sabkhas* (salt flats). The coastline is home to the most densely populated, salt-resistant mangrove habitat in Qatar. It is a popular spot for bird watching, kayaking, and fishing.

Hey, look at that turtle!
Cool!
Sea-turtles are known to regularly nest on this beach during late spring and early summer.

AL WAKRAH: A city in eastern Qatar, just south of Doha. The Wakrah Souq is a maze of alleyways and courtyards, full of aged clay structures, traditional architecture, a mosque and stables, and shops selling everything from honey, spices, and dates to perfumes and souvenirs. The beach is just minutes away from the souq and city center.

DAY
4

MESAIEED'S SAND DUNES: The natural formation of sand dunes make Mesaieed a popular tourist attraction for adventure seekers. A dune is a hill of loose sand in different shapes and sizes, formed by interaction with the flow of air or water.

ZEKREET: Part of northwestern Qatar. The area is largely uninhabited and is known for its large escarpments, with pillars and mushroom-like limestone formations. Zekreet was once known as "Film City" because the set for a popular show was built here.

DAY
6

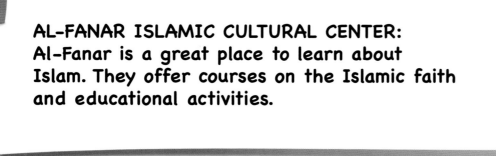

AL-FANAR ISLAMIC CULTURAL CENTER:
Al-Fanar is a great place to learn about Islam. They offer courses on the Islamic faith and educational activities.

TIME TO SAY GOODBYE...

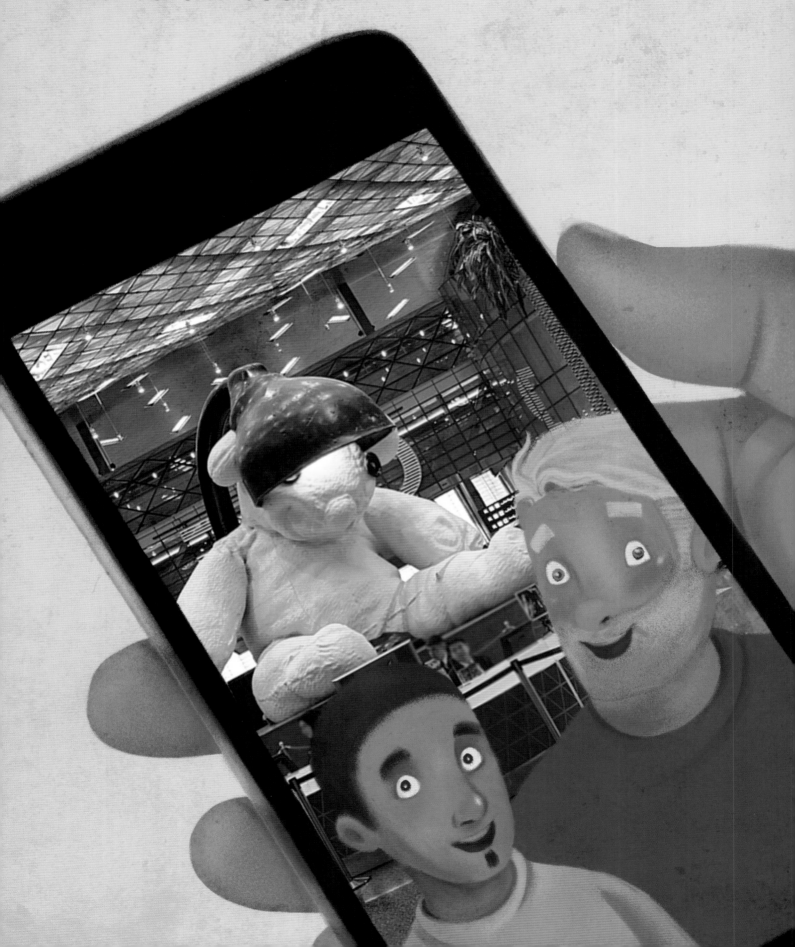

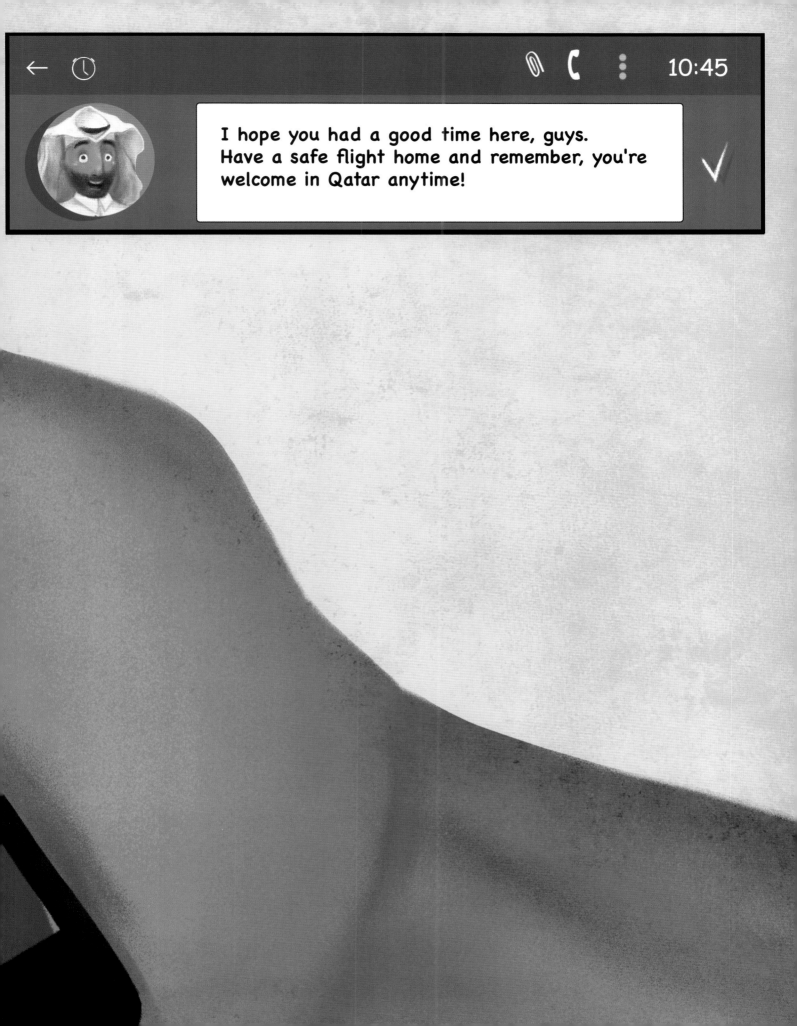

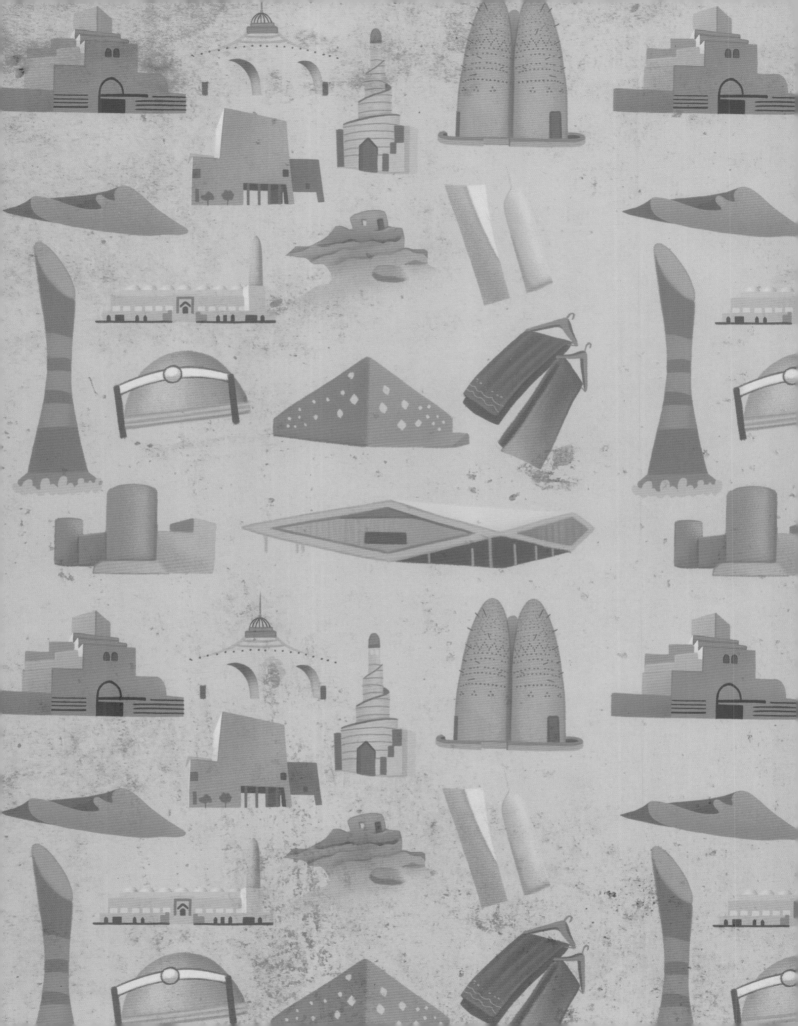